The Not-So Merry-Go-Round

Chapter One
As Slow As A Slug................... page 5

Chapter Two
A Secret Plan .... page 10

Chapter Three
Look Out! Meddlers About! .... page 17

Chapter Four
The Very-Merry-Go-Round......... page 24

Written by
Maureen Haselhurst

Illustrated by
Claudia Venturini

Meet the Meddlers

When something blows up,
when something breaks down,
look out – the Meddlers
are messing around!

Name: Professor Kybosh
Job: Teaches the art of meddling
Likes: Making clever plans and
singing rhymes
Dislikes: Cheeky children and pets

Name: Jinx
Job: Assistant to Professor
Kybosh
Likes: Being a star pupil
and bossing Spike around
Dislikes: Getting things wrong

Name: Spike
Job: Junior Assistant to
Professor Kybosh
Likes: His pet, Botch
Dislikes: Being bossed
around by his sister, Jinx

Name: Botch
Job: Fetches and carries
meddling tools
Likes: Spike
Dislikes: Being left out
of things

MABEL MOODY'S MERRY-GO-ROUND

Not-so-

4

Chapter One
As Slow As A Slug

Merry-go-rounds should be fun.
They should have bright lights
and loud music, and whizz
around so fast that you get dizzy.

Mabel Moody's merry-go-round
wasn't fun at all. It had dim
lights and mournful music, and it
turned round at a slug's speed.

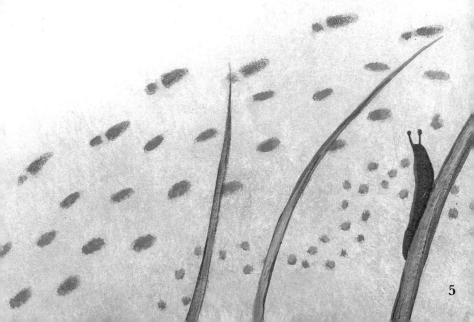

Hardly anyone went on the ride.

"It's *sooo* boring!" people complained.

"Well, that's too bad because I'm not going to change it," Mabel Moody grumbled moodily.

Little did she know that four
tiny spies had heard everything.
If Mabel Moody wouldn't change
things, then they would. They
were the Meddlers!

Meddlers are secretive little people. Their job is to make mischief and they are experts at it.

Professor Kybosh and his two assistants, Jinx and Spike, had moved into a cosy hidey-hole in the merry-go-round. Mabel Moody had no idea they were there.

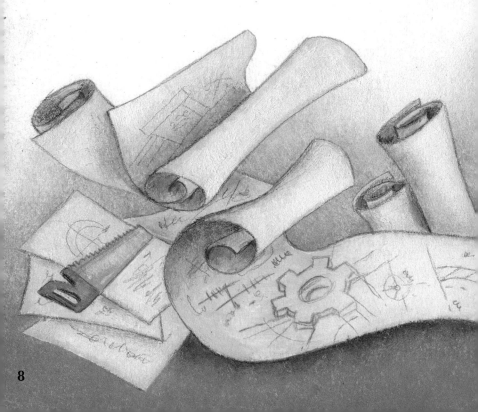

Chapter Two
A Secret Plan

"Now, pay attention," said Professor Kybosh. "I've got a brilliant idea for a mega-meddle." He whispered his secret plan.

Wow! What a meddle! It would give Mabel Moody the shock of her life.

"Knockout!" said Jinx in amazement.

"Do you think you can do it?" asked the Professor.

"You bet we can!" shouted Spike, eagerly.

HOW TO MESS WITH
A MERRY-GO-ROUND

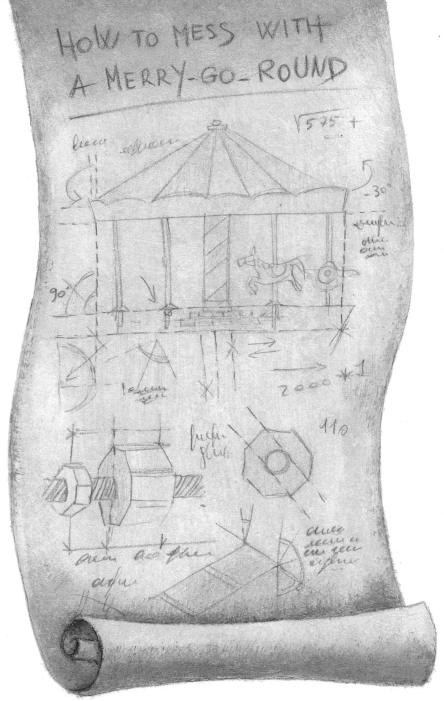

Professor Kybosh wagged his finger at Spike.

"I want this job done properly, Spike. You are careless and your mischief is not up to scratch. Now, watch what Jinx does. She's my star pupil."

"I'll keep an eye on him, Professor," said Jinx.

"Which means she'll boss me around," Spike whispered to Botch.

"And I don't want Botch to work on this meddle," said Professor Kybosh.

"But ..." Spike objected.

"No!" said the Professor firmly. "Botch will distract you."

13

When he saw Spike's disappointed face and Botch's lowered eyes, the Professor felt a bit mean. To cheer them up, he began to sing in a very cracked voice.

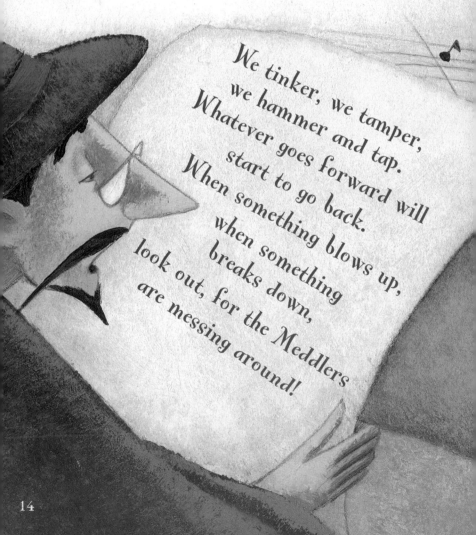

We tinker, we tamper,
we hammer and tap.
Whatever goes forward will
start to go back.
When something blows up,
when something
breaks down,
look out, for the Meddlers
are messing around!

Chapter Three
Look Out! Meddlers About!

It was nearly midnight and the not-so-merry-go-round was in darkness. Jinx and Spike picked up their tool kits and crept out of their hidey-hole. They had so much meddling to do and so little time in which to do it. They had to complete the job before it got light.

"Let's get meddling," said Jinx. With a whoop, they set to work.

They crawled through pipes, bounced on springs, swung on horses' tails and bungee-jumped on wires.

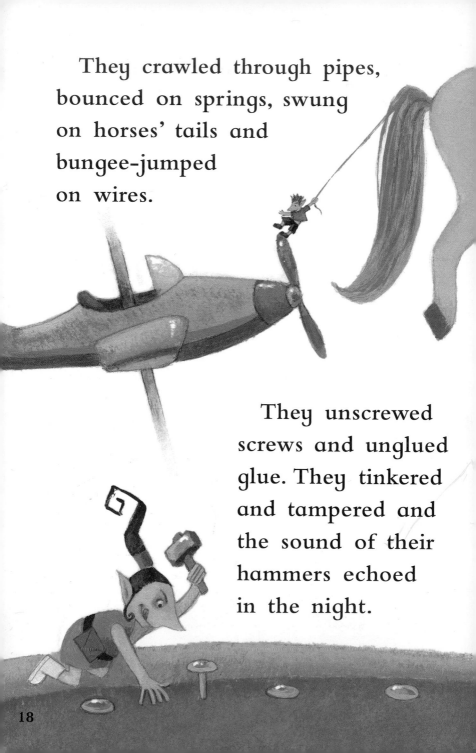

They unscrewed screws and unglued glue. They tinkered and tampered and the sound of their hammers echoed in the night.

"This is fun," giggled Spike. "I wish Botch was here."

"Shh!" said Jinx. "Someone's coming! Hide!"

There was the sound of
stomping footsteps and a pair of
huge feet appeared.

"Who's there?"

It was Mabel Moody's voice! Something rushed out of the darkness and grabbed at her shoelaces. Botch!

"What's going on?" demanded
Mabel Moody as she tripped and
tumbled over. Botch had tied her
shoelaces together!

"Run for it!" yelled Jinx.

"Well, how did it go?" asked Professor Kybosh as they scurried into the hidey-hole.

"Knockout!" they panted, and crossed their fingers.

Chapter Four
The Very-Merry-Go-Round

The next morning the Meddlers waited to see if their meddling had worked. But nothing seemed to have changed. The not-so-merry-go-round had dim lights and mournful music, and it still turned round at a slug's speed. The few children on it looked *sooo* bored.

Professor Kybosh looked cross. "What's happened?" he snapped. "Why hasn't the meddle worked?"

Then, without warning, there was a flurry of sparks and the merry-go-round went crazy. Loud music blasted out, bright disco lights flashed. The horses pranced and the planes zoomed around.

Round and round the
merry-go-round whizzed
and the children hung on,
screaming with excitement.
What a ride! What a meddle!

ERRY-GO-ROUND

Mabel Moody was puzzled. Who had been fooling around with her ride? She would get even with whoever it was!

Soon there was a long line of children wanting to ride on the very-merry-go-round. Mabel Moody's cashbox was full. Maybe things weren't so bad after all.

Mabel Moody wouldn't have been so pleased if she knew that four little people were riding free of charge. The Meddlers rode on the very-merry-go-round until they were dizzy with excitement.

"It was a brilliant meddle after all," giggled Jinx.

"Yes, but can Botch come next time?" asked Spike, and he winked at Jinx.

"Perhaps," said Professor Kybosh, smiling his crafty smile. "And speaking of next time, let's pack up and get moving. We've got a lot more meddling to do!"